Hare B&B

For Sydney Kalef, who has fed and sheltered so many.
~B.R. & B.P.

re B&B

written by **Bill Richardson**
&
illustrated by **Bill Pechet**

Her name was Harriet, but everyone called her Harry. Harry was an only child.

Then, unexpectedly, her mother had identical septuplets.

"Seven's a lot of work," said her father.

"Harry will help," said her mother.

Harry did.

She warmed bottles and changed nappies.
She got the babies up in the morning and tucked
them in at night. She told them stories and gave
them piggyback rides.

Harry loved her brothers and sisters. Their names
were Barry and Perry and Mary and Larry and
Jerry and Carrie.

Oh, and also Terry.

One day, Harry took Barry,
Perry, Mary, Larry, Jerry, Carrie,
and also Terry for a long walk in their large pram.

When they came home, a police officer was waiting.

Harry said, "What's wrong?"

"It's your parents," said the constable.

The news was bad.

A coyote had come knocking. This coyote
was a master of disguise. She was dressed
as an encyclopedia salesman.

Harry's mother and father, who prized education,
let her in.

That was that.

Harry was distraught. She said, "Why them? Why us? Why here? Why now?"

"Sometimes," the constable said, "bad things happen to good rabbits."

"We are not rabbits," said Harry. "We are hares.
And now, we are alone."

That night, Harry gathered the septuplets
for a meeting.

"We may be orphans, but we are still a family," she
said. "To keep our home, we must earn money."

"But how?" asked the little ones.

"Mama's and Papa's room is empty. We can take
in paying guests. We'll offer a bed at night and
breakfast in the morning. We'll be a Hare B&B.
I can prepare the breakfast. Each of you must do
something to help."

"I can dust," said Barry.

"I can vacuum," said Perry.

"I can wash dishes," said Mary.

"I can dry dishes," said Larry.

"I can launder linens," said Jerry.

"I can hang them on the line," said Carrie.

"I can entertain our guests with soothing music,"
said Terry, who was learning to play the harp.

Some of Harry's best friends were birds.

They advertised by twitter.

Guests arrived.

There was a squirrel, attending a high school reunion.

There was a skunk who looked like trouble, but was perfectly jovial.

And so on.

Variations on a Theme
by Terry

They all liked the Hare B&B.

The birds tweeted their good reviews.

"Scrumptious breakfast!"

"Comfy bed!"

"Soothing harp music!"

And so on.

HARP RECITAL

by

Terry

TONIGAT @ 7PM.

PROGRAM:

• FOREST GLADE by HARETOK
• HARP CONCERTO in B FLAT
        by SIGURD LEVERETZ
• VARIATIONS ON A THEME
        by Terry

TICKETS GOING
    FAST!
BOOK NOW!!!...

It was a success.

One evening, quite late, there came a knock
on the door. Harry answered. On the porch was
a homely rabbit.

"May I help you?" said Harry.

"I hope so. I'm going to my sister's wedding. I'm the maid of honour. I thought I could make the journey in a single day, but it's getting dark. May I stay at your Hare B&B?"

"Yes," said Harry, "our room is available."

"Thank you," smiled the unappealing rabbit, showing her yellow teeth. "We hares must stick together."

Harry was surprised. She knew her rabbits from her hares. This was no hare. Watching their guest walk upstairs, Harry suspected this was no rabbit, either.

"Your room," said Harry.

"Perfect," said the appalling rabbit.

"Breakfast in bed is at 7 sharp," said Harry.

"I can hardly wait," said the misbegotten rabbit. She burped. Her breath smelled of meat and barbecue sauce.

"Good night," said Harry. She closed the door.

Something was amiss.

Harry put her eye to the keyhole.

She watched the hideous rabbit remove her long,
rabbity ears, then her pink, rabbity nose, then her
cotton-puff, rabbity tail.

Harry had seen enough.

She woke the septuplets.

They made a plan.

The next morning, at 7 sharp, Harry knocked on the guest-room door.

"Come in!" croaked the beastly rabbit.

Harry entered. On a tray she carried a pitcher and a bowl.

"Is that my breakfast?" said the horrid rabbit, who looked truly dreadful.

"It is," said Harry. "And here are my seven little brothers and sisters to meet you."

They crowded around.

TICKLE POWDER

"Goodness!" said the grisly rabbit. "Aren't you the dearest things! Don't you all look sweet enough to eat?"

She chuckled. Drool dribbled.

"And all orphans," said Harry. "We lost our parents to a coyote who was a master of disguise."

"The villain!" said the monstrous rabbit, with great feeling. "Come closer, darlings, and call me 'Auntie'. Come very, very close and give Auntie a hug."

"May we, Harry?" asked the septuplets.

"You may," said Harry.

And did they hug her?

Well. Not exactly.

Barry and Perry
 jumped on the revolting rabbit and
tickled her till she roared.

Mary and Larry jumped on the repugnant rabbit
and pulled off both her ears.

Jerry and Carrie jumped on the repulsive rabbit and pulled off her nose and her tail.

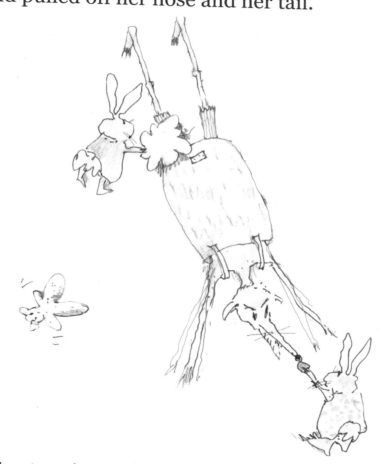

"Why Auntie, you're no hare and you're no rabbit, either! You're a big old coyote."

"Curse you," she snarled, and tried to grab them and gobble them up. But she couldn't. Terry had tied up her hands and feet with harp strings.

"And now," said Harry, "it's time for breakfast."

In the jug Harry had molasses, which she poured on top of the coyote.

"Arooooo!" howled the coyote, who prized cleanliness, and was now a sticky mess.

In the bowl, Harry had feathers, which she dumped onto the molasses.

"Achoooo!" sneezed the coyote, who was allergic to plumage.

The kerfuffle was so loud the constable stopped to investigate.

"Save me!"cried the coyote, who was thoroughly miserable. "Take me to jail where I'll be safe."

But the constable, who prized open doors over locked ones, had a different idea.

They escorted the coyote to the bus station.

They secured for her a sandwich and a one-way ticket to the distant riverside town of Alias-on-Grill, famous for its exquisite barbecue restaurants and plentiful costume shops.

"Perhaps there," said the constable, "you'll lead a life that brings more happiness than harm."

"Perhaps," said the coyote, who was unaccustomed to feeling so sore before noon and wondered if a change of direction might be in order.

The little ones were left feeling jittery. The world, they understood, was a dangerous place.

"Be calm," said Harry. "Remember, there is nothing a smart hare with a good plan cannot accomplish. We must move forward. We must love each other as much as we can. We cannot be fearful every time someone comes to the door."

The bell rang.

A new guest had arrived.

He looked like a duck.

He walked like a duck.

Harry was pretty sure a duck was what he was.

Bill Richardson and Bill Pechet live in Vancouver, B.C. They both love cabbage.

This book was designed by Veselina Tomova of Vis-à-vis Graphics, St. John's, NL,
and printed in Canada.

978-1-927917381

Running the Goat, Books & Broadsides gratefully acknowledges support for its
publishing activities from Newfoundland and Labrador's Department of Tourism,
Culture, Arts and Recreation through its Publishers Assistance Program;
the Canadian Department of Heritage and Multiculturalism through the Canada
Book Fund; and the Canada Council for the Arts,
through its Literary Publishing Projects Fund.

Newfoundland Labrador

Canada Council Conseil des arts
for the Arts du Canada

Funded by the Government of Canada
Financé par le gouvernement du Canada | Canada

For your tummy or garden!